This is serious!!!!

DO NOT READ THIS BOOK or you will be punished. Big time. No Joke!

Here's some of the real bad things that could happen to YOU —

1. You'll be forced to eat vegetables with weird names that come from another country.

2. You'll be forced to stick a wiggly bug in your ear.

3. Ninja cats will sneak up on you in the dark.

4. You will always be "it" in ANY game.

5. You'll get chicken pox TWICE!

6. Just for Boys — You'll have to kiss a girl with braces.
   Just for Girls — You'll have to kiss a snake on the lips.

There's more bad stuff, but it's just too horrible to write down.

You better stop reading NOW!!!

This is your LAST warning!!!!

Islandport Press
P.O. Box 10
247 Portland Street
Yarmouth, Maine 04096

books@islandportpress.com
www.islandportpress.com
First published in May 2014

ISBN: 978-1-939017-16-1
Library of Congress Control Number: 2013922646
Dean L. Lunt, publisher
Karen Hoots, book designer

ISLANDPORT PRESS

YARMOUTH • MAINE

Adventures in Vacationland

by
Mark Scott Ricketts

*A story based on and featuring
selections from
Commander Joe Livingston's
super top-secret journal*

JOE'S
JOURNAL

ISLANDPORT PRESS

SPLOOF! Chocolate milk shot through Joe Livingston's nose when he learned his auntie was missing in the wilds of Vacationland. Joe needed to rescue her! (After he cleaned milk off the wall, of course.)

POST CARD

JULY
MAINE

Joe -
Help! This place is wack-a-doodle. I'm all turned around. I need you to f⋯ ⋯ore things g⋯ ⋯tier
Love,
Auntie

FAMOUS EXPLORER
MISSING

← HAVE YOU SEEN MY AUNTIE?

I assembled a crackerjack team of experts to help me find my auntie.

ME

"COMMANDER JOE"
Explorer, dare-taker, rock thrower, monkey bars climber, and worm handler.

DAD

"THE WHEEL MAN"
Top-notch driver and radio knob twister.

MOM

"THE SCOUT"
Really good map reader and snack packer.

LT. SPOT

"THE WILD CARD"
Second-in-command. Specializes in baring teeth, growling, and face licking.

Commander Joe gathered his rescue team and raced off to find Auntie.

Native tribesmen stopped the rescue team at the gates of Vacationland. Joe needed to win the right to enter their Moose Kingdom ... in COMBAT!

The Moose King challenged Joe to a STARING CONTEST. Joe knew all the tricks. The moment Joe saw the king struggling to keep his eyes open, he unleashed his GOOFY FACE. The king laughed so hard, he BLINKED. Joe won!

The gates began to rise.

The Moose King warned Joe that many hair-raising obstacles and spine-tingling pitfalls awaited them in the deep, dark jungles and stormy waters of Vacationland.

The king's warnings didn't scare Joe. He was prepared for ADVENTURE!

Joe and his team hadn't traveled more than a few miles when they bumped into a wicked big problem: a Maine Coon Cat!

That kitty was JUMBO-SIZE!

He was what Joe's grandpa would call a WHOPPER! There was NO WAY to get around him.

The fat cat was catching some rays, and refused to budge from his sunny spot.

Mom (the Scout) sprang into action. Using her special explorer maps and fancy gadgets, she found a hidden, but more dangerous, road.

IT'S A LITTLE OUT OF THE WAY,

BUT IT CAN GET US WHERE WE'RE GOING.

MAYBE.

I HOPE.

The roads were rocky and cracked. They had steep hills and deep dips. It was one rough ride.

The car swerved, wiggled, flipped ...

shook, hopped, dipped ...

flopped ...

shimmied, and twitched.

Joe felt like he was riding a crazy, runaway roller coaster.

The sights were awesome. I saw things in Vacationland you won't see anywhere else. I saw a lot of SPOOKY stuff, too!

SPOT!

Spot met a girl blackfly. They didn't get along. She bites.

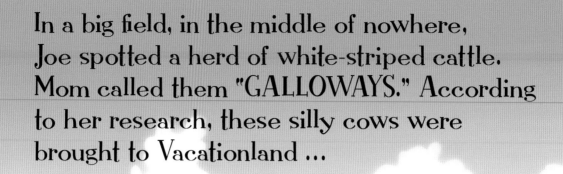

In a big field, in the middle of nowhere,
Joe spotted a herd of white-striped cattle.
Mom called them "GALLOWAYS." According
to her research, these silly cows were
brought to Vacationland ...

... all the way from Scotland.

Joe and his team didn't stop for a closer look ...

Blueberry pie

... mostly because those loony cows started tossing blueberry pies at them.

Dad, a tough-as-nails wheel man, swerved before the car got completely GOOPED UP with icky blueberry slime.

They shot off like a ROCKET!

Finally, Joe and his team reached the ocean.
TA DAH!

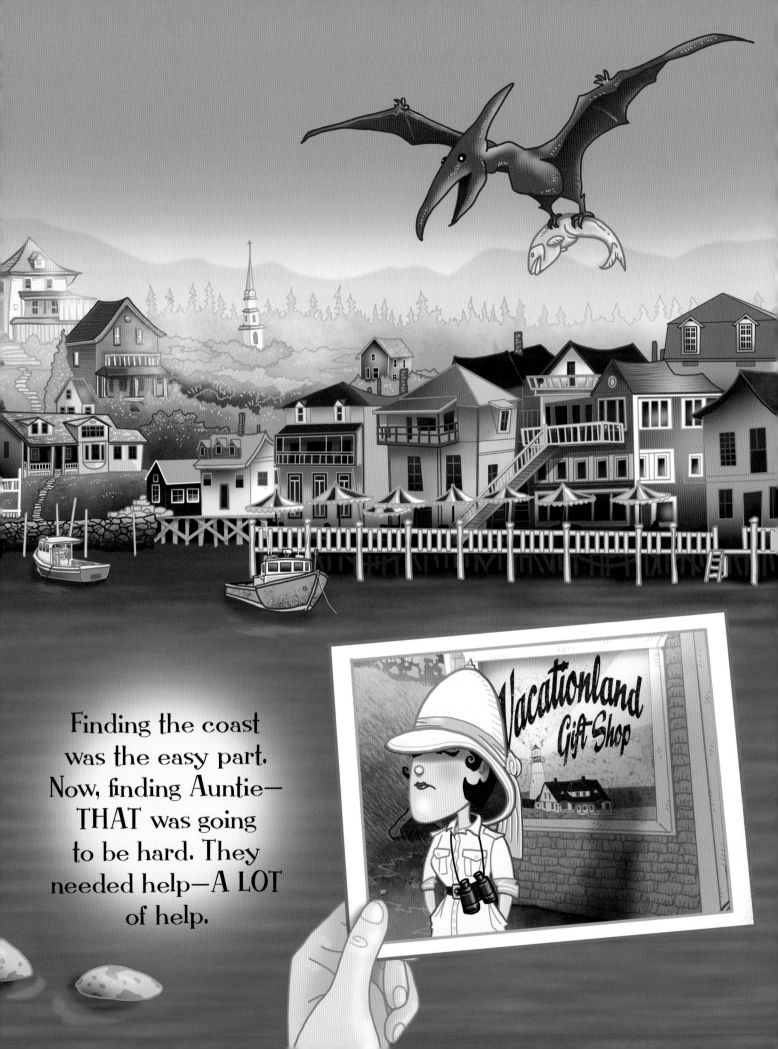

Finding the coast was the easy part. Now, finding Auntie—THAT was going to be hard. They needed help—A LOT of help.

Vacationland Gift Shop

Joe met a sentry who rarely moved from his station. He smelled like stinky fish, but he had important information about Auntie's whereabouts.

Joe and his team stopped to eat at a local seafood joint. With all the people there, surely one of them knew something about his missing auntie.

Joe met an old sea captain who offered to help.

The Lobster POUND

Captain Chester →

Captain Chester knew everything about Vacationland.
He knew every beautiful nook and every
scary cranny.

Captain Chester warned Joe that the search would be
dangerous—especially if they came face-to-claw
with the terrible sea monster known as ...

Captain Chester knew of a tower where you could see nearly everything and everyone in Vacationland. It was worth a shot, so they set sail for Huffin Puffin Island.

Sailing with Captain Chester was crazy FUN!

We battened down the hatches.

We hoisted the mainsail.

We met a giant octopus.

We did a lot of swashbuckling, too.

DAD GOT SEASICK

Huffin Puffin Island

Lupine Forest

Blinken Headlight X

100 200 300 400 500 600 700 800 900

Joe thought the trip to Huffin Puffin Island took FOREVER. And once they arrived, they still had a long way to go.

A rowboat ride.

A climb up a rocky shore loaded with pushy puffins.

GO HOME!

And a hike through the Great Lupine Forest, with beady little puffin eyes watching their every move.

LUPINE   ME

When the team finally emerged from the forest, they spotted the tower of all towers ...

the Blinken Head Light!

At the tip-top of the world's most crookedest and gnarliest lighthouse, an extra-special, hi-def, 3D telescope provided Joe with a bird's-eye view of Vacationland.

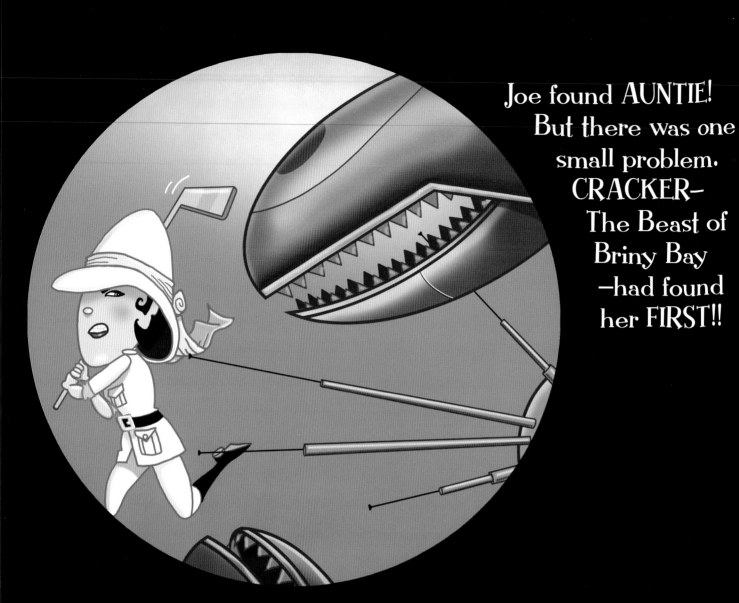

Joe found AUNTIE!
But there was one
small problem.
CRACKER—
The Beast of
Briny Bay
—had found
her FIRST!!

RUFF!

Auntie was in BIG trouble.
So we rushed off to rescue her.

Captain Chester called the
Vacationland police for help.

MAYDAY!!!

Just when CRACKER looked
unbeatable, the MOOSE POLICE
unveiled their secret
weapon and blasted
Cracker with jets of
hot melted butter.

Slowly the globs of goopy butter began to clog the mechanical lobster's robotic guts, springs, and gears.

Cracker sparked and sputtered to a STOP.

The battle was over. Cracker was down for the count. But who created him?*

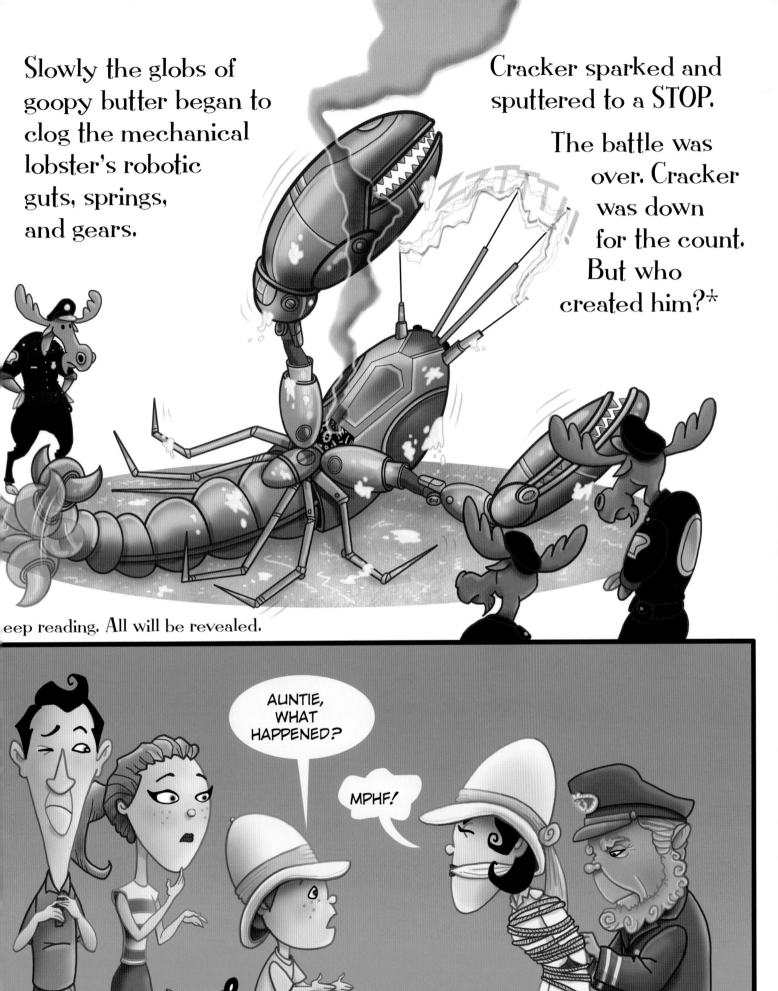

...eep reading. All will be revealed.

AUNTIE, WHAT HAPPENED?

MPHF!

THE SALTY DOUG STORY

Salty Doug was not only a lobsterman, he was also an inventor.

He created special machines to help him catch lobsters in Briny Bay.

But Salty Doug didn't much like sharing the bay with other lobstermen.

So he came up with a way to keep all the lobsters in Briny Bay just for himself.

Salty Doug built
a monster
to scare away
boats from
Briny Bay.

When my auntie discovered
Salty Doug's plan, he got real
mad and tied her up.

But my team and I showed
up, and there was a BIG fight!

In the end, the monster
was destroyed and Auntie
was set free.

Salty Doug did not live
happily ever after.

Joe's auntie was safe. Joe was really happy. (Well, he would have been happier if he'd been eating ice cream when he found her, but he was still really, really happy!)

MY HERO!

Mark Scott Ricketts is a Maine-based,
Arkansas-born writer/illustrator who has
enjoyed national success in advertising, graphic
novels, and comic books, including as author
of several Iron Man comics. Ricketts published
A Flatlander's Guide to Maine with
Islandport Press in 2013.

DO NOT READ!!

JOE'S JOURNAL

FOR MY EYES ONLY!

DANGER!

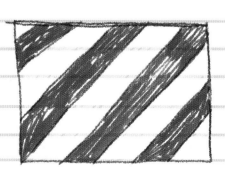

KEEP OUT!